This Little Tiger book belongs to:

_____

_____

_____

For Pete and Shirley Davies, with all my love x
~ S M

For Mum, Dad and Rachel
~ C G

LITTLE TIGER PRESS LTD,
an imprint of the Little Tiger Group
1 Coda Studios, 189 Munster Road, London SW6 6AW
Imported into the EEA by Penguin Random House Ireland,
Morrison Chambers, 32 Nassau Street, Dublin D02 YH68
www.littletiger.co.uk

First published in Great Britain 2020
This edition published 2021

Text by S. Marendaz
Illustrations by Carly Gledhill
Text and illustrations copyright © Little Tiger Press Ltd 2020

THE BEDTIME BOOK

S MARENDAZ

CARLY GLEDHILL

LITTLE TIGER

LONDON

It was a cool, still night and
Frank was cuddled up in bed.

His eyes closed.

He snuggled under his blanket.

He was just about to fall asleep when . . .

"Frank! Frank!" It was Mouse.
Frank opened one sleepy eye.
"What is it, Mouse?"
"Someone has taken my bedtime book!"
Poor Mouse was very upset. "It's my
favourite."

"Oh dear," said Frank. "Maybe
your book is just hiding somewhere?"
   "But I put it outside my flowerpot ready
for bedtime," squeaked Mouse. "And when
I went home it had GONE."

Frank went with Mouse to her flowerpot at once.

Scurry,

scurry,

scurry.

Pant,

pant,

pant.

Just as Mouse said, there
was no book outside.

"Your book HAS gone,"
agreed Frank.

"But what's this?"
Sniff . . . sniff . . . "It's a trail!"
Sniff!
Sniff!
Sniff!

Frank and Mouse followed the trail up
. . . down . . . and around, until at last
it led them to . . .

"Bella! Did you take Mouse's book?"

"Hmm," said Bella. "Did it have a blue cover?"
"Yes! Yes! That's my book!" Mouse was very excited.
"Oh dear me," said Bella. "I thought it was a lost book! I put it in a nice clearing by the flowerbeds so it could be spotted."

"Quick! We'll find it, Mouse!"
cried Frank.
They all rushed over to the
clearing at once.

Scurry,

scurry,

scurry.

Pant,

pant,

pant.

But when they got to the clearing,
Mouse's book wasn't there.

They looked high.

And they looked low.

But they couldn't find
Mouse's book anywhere.

"My book is lost forever!"
Poor Mouse was very upset.

Bella and Frank patted
Mouse's back kindly.

"Book?" asked a voice.
It was Owl. "I found a
book! Does it have shiny
stars on the cover?"

"Yes! Yes! That's my book!" said Mouse.
"Oh dear me," said Owl. "I took it to
Baby Hedgehog. I thought he would like
a bedtime story."

"Quick! We'll get it,
Mouse!" cried Frank.

But Mouse shook her head. "I can't take it back from Baby Hedgehog. The book will make him very happy."

She walked sadly away to bed.

Back in his bed, Frank snuggled
his nose under the blanket.
   He closed his eyes.
   But he couldn't sleep.
   "Mouse will be sad without her favourite
book," thought Frank. "She was so kind to
share it with Baby Hedgehog."

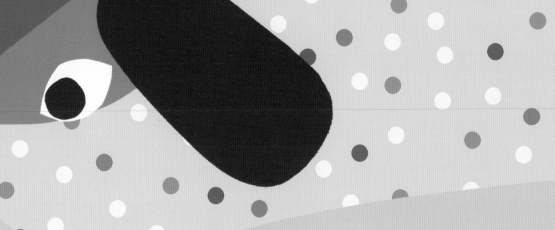

Suddenly, Frank had a brilliant idea.

He rushed to Mouse's
flowerpot at once.

Pant,
pant,
pant.

"Mouse! Mouse! Are you awake?"

"I've brought you my favourite bedtime book, Mouse," said Frank. "I thought we could read it together."
Mouse was very pleased. The two friends settled down, and Frank started reading.

The story sounded very familiar.

Mouse looked at the front cover.
It was blue, with shiny stars.

"Frank! That's MY book! We have
the same favourite book!"

"We DO? How about that!"

So Mouse and Frank read their favourite book
all the way to the end . . .
And together they fell fast asleep
under the starry sky.

Snore,

snore,

snore.